PUFFIN BOOKS

the Diary of Dennis THE MENACE
The Great Escape!

Collect all of DENNIS's diaries!

The Diary of Dennis the Menace

The Diary of Dennis the Menace: Beanotown Battle

The Diary of Dennis the Menace: Rollercoaster Riot!

The Diary of Dennis the Menace: Bash Street Bandit!

The Diary of Dennis the Menace: Canine Carnage

Other books by Steven Butler:

The Wrong Pong

The Wrong Pong: Holiday Hullabaloo

The Wrong Pong: Singin' in the Drain

The Wrong Pong: Troll's Treasure

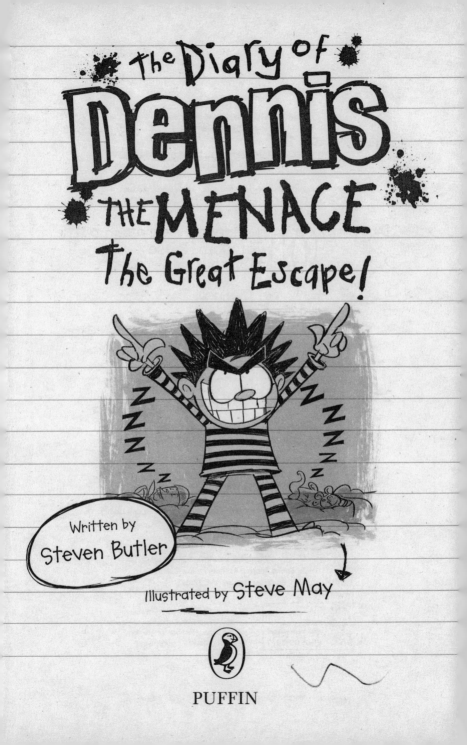

The Diary of Dennis THE MENACE
The Great Escape!

Written by
Steven Butler

Illustrated by Steve May

PUFFIN

PUFFIN BOOKS

UK | USA | Canada | Ireland | Australia
India | New Zealand | South Africa

Puffin Books is part of the Penguin Random House group of companies
whose addresses can be found at global.penguinrandomhouse.com.

www.penguin.co.uk   www.puffin.co.uk   www.ladybird.co.uk

Penguin
Random House
UK

First published 2016
003

Written by Steven Butler
Illustrated by Steve May
Copyright © DC Thomson & Co. Ltd, 2016
The Beano ® ©, Dennis the Menace ® © and associated
characters are TM and © DC Thomson & Co. Ltd, 2016
All rights reserved

The moral right of the author, illustrator
and copyright holders has been asserted

Set in Soupbone
Designed by Mandy Norman
Printed in Great Britain by Clays Ltd, St Ives plc

A CIP catalogue record for this book is available from the British Library

ISBN: 978–0–141–35586–3

All correspondence to:
Puffin Books, Penguin Random House Children's
80 Strand, London WC2R 0RL

MIX
Paper from
responsible sources
FSC® C018179

Penguin Random House is committed to a
sustainable future for our business, our readers
and our planet. This book is made from Forest
Stewardship Council® certified paper.

For Matt Beadle,

a true Menace at heart.

I know he's causing

mischief somewhere . . .

Hold on to your bonces,

my Menacing Mates.

Your **BRILLIANT** menacing leader, **RULER OF ROCK** and **INTERNATIONAL MENACE OF MYSTERY** is about to tell you something that will make your heads rocket off your shoulders with surprise. If you know anything about me and my **MEGA** diaries, this could be the most **SHOCKING** thing you've ever heard!

You're going to think I've gone **round the twist** when you see what I'm about to write, my Menacing Pals . . .

I can picture it now . . .

You'll turn the page, read what's on it and think,
'Dennis the Menace has had his brains scrambled!

HE'S GONE POTTY!

HE'S STARK RAVING

BONKERS!'

Are **YOU** ready?

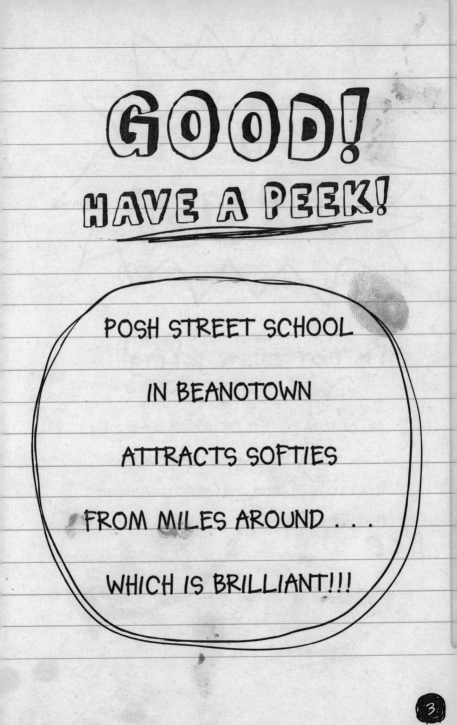

IT'S TRUE!

I'm not even joking!

You're thinking that I'm playing a menacing trick on you, but look what was on the front page of Mum and Dad's newspaper this morning . . .

DOES YOUR CHILD HAVE WHAT IT TAKES TO MAKE IT INTO THE FINEST SCHOOL THE COUNTRY HAS TO OFFER?

Well, now the families of Beanotown can find out.

Today the Mayor announced that Posh Street School, the elite boarding academy for the EXTREMELY WELL-BEHAVED and SUPER SMART, is offering a scholarship to one child.

The *Beanotown Bugle* is certain the most polite and well-mannered children from the finest families in Beanotown will want to take advantage of this exclusive opportunity!

IT'S AMAZING!

I DON'T THINK I'VE EVER FELT SO HAPPY!!!

Haha! Come on, admit it . . . you're suddenly feeling completely **TERRIFIED** that your leader, **THE PRANKMASTER GENERAL** himself, has joined the wafty, booky, boring, **BUM-FACED**, whingey, whiney, devious, SMARMING hordes of SOFTIES!!!!

THIS IS YOU!

How could Dennis be excited? This is AWFUL!

Oh, all right . . . I'll put you out of your misery before you burst into tears and throw this book in the bin, screaming,

'Dennis!

NoOOOooOOOOOoo!!!!

HE'S GONE LOOP-DE-LOOP!'

The article from the newspaper didn't end there. **AGH! I CAN'T WAIT FOR YOU TO READ IT.** This could be the best news in the history of best, **BEST,**

BESTEST NEWS . . .

EVER!!!

Brace yourselves.

To CELEBRATE THE CENTENARY OF Posh Street School, Headmistress Miss Phyllida Snoot will reserve a single place on the register for one pupil from Bash Street School. An intelligence test will be carried out this week and the lucky, high-achieving child who gets the best marks will be immediately transferred to Posh Street School and will receive the most expensive education a brilliant young student could ever hope for.

The name of the winning Bash Street School pupil will be announced in a gala assembly on Friday.

IT'S TOO BRILLIANT!

Anyone with half a brain knows that no one at Bash Street School gets higher marks than Walter. Don't get me wrong – he isn't as BRAIN-TASTICALLY MEGA-MINDED as me . . . obviously . . . but our teacher, Mrs Creecher, LOVES HIM! She never fails to give Walter top grades and he ALWAYS aces her boring, BORING, BORING history tests . . . ALWAYS!

If this is the first time you've read one of my AMAZING menacing manuals, you probably don't know about my whopping great SMARMER of an arch-enemy.

BUM-FACE ALERT!!!

Let me tell you, my Trainee Menaces, that Walter is the whiniest, bookiest, most boring BUM-FACE in all of ~~Beanotown~~ ~~the~~ ~~World~~ THE UNIVERSE!!!

Just call me Sir Smarmsalot!

But one thing's for sure: when it comes to schoolwork and sums and TESTS . . .

HE CAN'T LOSE!

Walter loves taking exams. They're his favourite hobby! While the rest of us are out having fun around Beanotown like proper Menaces should, Walter is always at home reading up on some **BRAIN-NUMBING** old such-'n'-such . . .

HAHA!

He's probably at home now reading *The Joy of Herb Gardens* or *Morris Dancing for Beginners.*

BLEEuuUrRGH!!!

At the end of this week, Posh Street School is sure to announce him as their winner and he'll be whisked off forever.

BYE-BYE, BUM-FACE!

The best part is I won't even have to see him skipping about outside school either! Posh Street School is a boarding school!! A BOARDING SCHOOL! Can you imagine actually wanting to live in school!?!?

IT'S MADNESS!

HAHA! It's great for us Menaces, though.

It means Bash Street School will be declared a

SOFTY-FREE ZONE!

MENACES WILL REIGN SUPREME!

Just think about it . . . with the leader of the Softies out of the way, Bash Street School could become **A MENACING UNIVERSITY!** I could take over and turn it into the **GREATEST** training academy for **PRANKMASTER GENERALS** there ever was!

It'll be my menacing masterpiece!

Who cares about all those Whingey—Wilfreds going to Posh Street School when there'll be an even bigger school for the coolest, most adventurous, **MOST MENACY KIDS IN THE WORLD** just a few streets away!

I'll be in charge and I'll call it Dennis's

COLLEGE OF CHAOS!

Or ... umm ...

EMPEROR MENAGE'S
MINISTRY
OF MAYHEM!

Yep! That one ...

Ha! Mrs Creecher won't know what to do with herself without her favourite prize pupil to smarm around her. I'll send her packing . . . and Headmaster too!

OH, WALTER! COME BACK!

WOE IS ME!

BUMFACE

BAS
STRE
SCHC

(ARTIST'S IMPRESSION)

Me, Curly, Pie Face and the Bash Street Kids
could be ruling the school in no time.

No more tests . . .

No more
homework . . .

And I'll get Olive the dinner lady to serve us
Slopper-Gnosher-Gut-Bustin' Burgers!
No more of her disgusting mush!

When we get to school tomorrow, you can bet Walter will be absolutely desperate to take the test. Ha! For once I wish him as much luck as possible. I hope he gets 100 out of 100! I hope he gets the HIGHEST mark in the history of high marks.

I certainly won't be studying tonight. Nope! Why on earth would I waste a whole evening doing something like that? I plan to get 0 out of 100 in the test. I'm not taking any chances.

Walter will be at home right now with his nose stuck in a book, studying, but not me . . . The only learning I'm going to do is finding out what the bottom of an EXTRA-MASSIVE bowl of DOUBLE FATTIES' DOUBLE-FAT ICE CREAM looks like.

DOUBLE FATTIES' DOUBLE-FAT ICE CREAM

BRILLIANT!

Catch you later, my TRAINEE MENACES.

Monday

7.30 a.m.: GOOD MORNING, WORLD!

Ah, I woke up in the best mood I think I've ever been in. I can already feel my life getting more and more Softy-free with every second that goes by. If I wasn't such a **MEGA-MENACE**, I think I might cry . . .

8.30 a.m.: And we're off! What did I tell

you, my Menacing Mates? I'd only just waved goodbye to my best dog-pal, Gnasher, at the garden gate when Walter came sprinting out of his house.

He was flapping about so much he looked like a demented rooster. _Haha!_

I suppose I can't blame him, though.

Going to a **SNOBBO** school like

Posh Street is every Softy's idea

of a dream come true and Walter

knows as well as anyone that

he'll get the highest marks in the

exam today. He must be practically

fainting with giddiness.

9 a.m.:

Looks like this Posh Street School test is a bit more serious than I thought, my Trainee Menaces. We've only just got to class and Mrs Creecher has already insisted we go straight to the school hall. Normally I'd be dreading this bit. **I HATE TESTS!** But today I couldn't be happier to get going. The quicker we start, the quicker Walter can get top marks and we never have to see his **BUM-FACE** again. Sigh . . .

<u>Here goes!</u> There are loads of tables set out in lines in the school hall and we all have to sit in total silence. **TOTAL SILENCE!?!?!** It's not going to be easy, my Menacing Mates, but making sure I get every question wrong is definitely worth it. I'm really, **REALLY, REALLY** going to concentrate . . .

Wish me luck . . .
or not . . .
HA!

QUESTION:

WHO IS THE GREATEST GENIUS IN ALL OF BEANOTOWN?

ME!!!

It's done, my Trainee Menaces.

The test took ages and there were what felt like zillions of questions, but I worked super hard and made sure I wrote down all the wrong answers. There's no chance that anyone is going to stand in Walter's way! He'll be packed off to Softy school for sure!

I wish you could have been there.
After we'd finished writing, Mrs
Creecher collected all the test
papers and clonkered off to her
office to mark them.

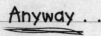

Teachers are so weird.
She looked even more excited about
marking the exam than Walter did
about taking it!

Anyway . . .

After lunch, Old Creech came back into the classroom, stood by her desk and got us to come up to the front one by one and collect our results. She made us all wait there, take our papers and hold them up for everyone else to see, and I know she only did it to try to embarrass me. Little did she know . . .

It all worked perfectly, my Trainee Menaces.

WALTER GOT THE
<u>HI</u>GHEST SCORE!

I knew he would.

AND . . . EVEN BETTER . . .
I GOT THE <u>LOWEST</u>!

There's **ABSOLUTELY** no way I'm ever going to have to get close enough to Posh Street School to even smell the **WHIFF OF SOFTY** that must stink up the corridors and classrooms in that place.

My test paper was a
MENACING MARVEL!

Have a look . . .

POSH  STREET

OYA ET LARDUM

SCHOOL ENTRY EXAM

Bash Street Student Name: **DENNIS**

1. Who was Leonardo da Vinci?

A. That wrinkly old man who invented **pizza** . . .
Or Mrs Creecher's **boyfriend** . . . Or both . . .

2. Complete the name of this world-famous wonder.
The Great Wall of . . . **BELGIUM!**

3. Name a story by the Brothers Grimm.

A. Attack of the **Bum-eating** Vacuum Cleaner.

4. Is a whale a fish or a mammal?

A. Neither . . . **It's a whale, STUPID!**

5. How many days are there in a normal year?

A. **Four hundred billion** and a half.

6. What is the answer to this sum: 4 + 5 − 1 =

A. Yellow!

7. What is the capital city of France?

A. Scotland.

8. Earth, Saturn, Pluto and Mars are the names of what?

A. Mrs Creecher's pet guinea pigs.

9. What food do giant pandas usually eat?

A. Slopper-Gnosher-Gut-Bustin' Burgers!

10. Name the seven colours of the rainbow.

A. Black, grey, brown, pink, bogey-green, mustard and white.

It couldn't have gone better, even if
I do say so myself.

Ahhh . . . life is good. Now all I have
to do is sit back and wait for Friday
when I'll wave goodbye to my archest
enemy **FOREVER**.

FOREVER!!!

FOREVER!

Forever!

FOREVER!

Forever!

I think that might be my new
favourite word . . .

Tuesday

3.30 p.m.: OK, my Menacing Mates, I've tried to be patient and wait for Friday, but it's **KILLING ME!** I never imagined it would be so difficult. It's like waiting for your birthday or the last day of school . . . OR **CHRISTMAS!**

I JUST CAN'T WAIT ANY MORE!

To make things worse, Walter is being even smarmier than usual and keeps skipping around school, saying things like . . .

UGH!

He's driving me mad. I know it's **FANTASTIC** that Walter's leaving Bash Street School, but I just wish he wasn't so pleased with himself. I mean, it's not like he actually, **ACTUALLY** beat me. Everyone knows I'm much smarter than that Wet-Lettuce and, if I'd wanted to, I could easily have got the highest mark in that stupid test . . . probably . . .

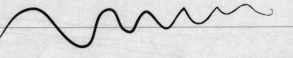

RIGHT, THAT'S IT!

WHY AM I MOPING ABOUT, WAITING FOR FRIDAY, WHEN I'VE GOT MEGA-MENACING PLANS TO MAKE? If I'm going to take over Bash Street School and **FINALLY** turn it into the headquarters of my **MENACING EMPIRE**, I need to stock up on some supplies.

Normally I'd just go down to the junkyard with Curly and Pie Face, but I've still got some pocket money left over and this is no ordinary situation. In moments like these, there's only one place I go for the finest-quality menacing goods . . . **Mr Har Har's Joke Shop!**

If your town is anything like Beanotown, there must be a **GREAT** joke shop nearby where you can get all your tricks and pranks and tools of the menacing trade.

Menacing Lesson no. 5611:

Always be sure to know where your nearest joke shop is. You never can tell when the opportunity for a spot of mischief will come your way and you MUST be well stocked up . . . all good Menaces are!

4 p.m.:

Check . . . check . . . This is Dennis,

INTERNATIONAL
MENACE OF MYSTERY,

reporting for duty. I'm coming to you live from

inside the funnest, craziest, noisiest shop of

them all.

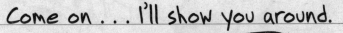

I love this place. Mr Har Har's really is the coolest shop in all of Beanotown. You can get anything here . . . and if you can't find what you want then it's not worth having.

Come on . . . I'll show you around.

43

4.27 p.m.:

All done . . . I've spent the last of my pocket money, but it was SO worth it. That's me all stocked up with fresh elastic for my catapult, soap that turns your hands black, sweets that taste like vomit . . . and what Menace can resist **FART PELLETS!?!?** These things will even outstink my little sister, **BEA!**

BEA: MEGA-FARTER!

BRILLIANT!

Wednesday

I've decided to put all this waiting around to good use because . . . it's **WET PLAYTIME!**

Any Menace worth their stripes HATES wet playtime. It's the worst kind there is. Just because of a teensy bit of wimbly-pimbly rain, Headmaster keeps us all inside like prisoners and forces us to stay in the classroom and read. **READ!?!?**

IT'S EVIL!!!

Well, not me, my Menacing Mates. I haven't got time today for books and reading and all that stuff. I've started my plans for turning Bash Street School into the Ministry of Mayhem.

Just imagine it . . .

First, I'd open all the big freezers in the school kitchen and let the slush and ice run out on to the floor until the whole place was an enormous ice rink.

Saucepan sledge

Endless supply of ice cream for eating on the go

FROST-TASTIC!

47

I'd turn all the taps on in Headmaster's loo (where he goes to read the newspaper and have a quick wee in peace) and make it the COOLEST swimming pool for dive-bombing and 'who can do the biggest fart bubble?' competitions. HA!

Fart bubbles

The footy field would become the main training ground for all the hundreds of menacing students.

Tree-climbing agility

Shooting gallery

POP!

Mega-fart training

49

And BEST of all . . .

The school hall would become my office . . .
no . . . MY **MENACING HUB!**
It's where I'd sit and invent genius new
menaces, while scoffing tubs of Double Fatties'
double-fat ice cream. I'd fill my hub with video
games and telly screens and loads of other
cool gadgets that the **PRANKMASTER**
GENERAL should have.

BUM FACE

MEGA-SIZE
GIANT
CATAPULT

Endless supply of
rotten tomatoes
for ammunition

ROTTEN
TOMATOES
'R
US™

ROTTEN
TOMATOES
'R
US™

DOUBLE
FATTIES'
DOUBLE FAT ICE CREAM

Thursday

10.20 a.m.: **UGH!** It's such a long time until FRIDAY and Walter's **STILL** skipping his way around the classroom with a smug look plastered across his **BUM-FACE**. It's enough to turn your stomach . . . Seeing his weaselly little grin makes me wish I **HAD** beaten him in the test. **Ha!** Imagine the look of shock on his face if that ever happened!

Still, there's nothing in the world that's worth being stuck in Posh Street School day and night, doing nothing but schoolwork, never going out to play around Beanotown, and having to spend all your time with hundreds of Softies for the rest of your life . . . not even the glory of defeating my archest enemy.

Walter's best snob-nosed pals, Bertie and
Dudley, haven't stopped crying since they
found out their leader is blasting off to
Planet Soggy Bottom. Even Mrs Creecher
seems really down in the dumps . . . HA!

Don't get me wrong: all that stuff is
hilarious. IT'S JUST TOO GOOD TO
BE TRUE, but . . . I . . . I . . .

I HATE WAITING!!!

Can't sleep . . .

Wide awake . . .

Even <u>Gnasher's</u> restless!

Well . . . actually that's probably down to the fact that he got into my school bag earlier and ate half a packet of fart pellets when me, Mum, Dad and Bea were eating dinner. He came downstairs, poor thing, and suddenly rocketed up to the ceiling, doing the longest run of the biggest blow-offs I've ever heard! The stink was unbelievable! We had to open every window in the house and run about flapping Mum's tea towels just to get rid of it.

Anyway, where was I? Oh yes . . . __UGH!__

I CAN'T SLEEP.

All this waiting is **SO BORING!**

If you haven't read any of my other MENACE-TASTIC diaries, you won't know about the devious mystery menaces, **evil librarians,**

endless BORING history tests, angry

zookeepers, flower festivals, Softy sleepovers

and trips to the countryside that I've had to

put up with over the past year. There were

times I felt sure I was a goner, but I'd happily

face them all again, and at the same time

too, if it meant that Friday would

hurry up and arrive.

GROOOOAAAAANNNNN!!!

Only one more sleep until I can put my Ministry of Mayhem plan into action. It's going to be the coolest thing EVER!

Maybe I'll try counting sheep to help me drift off . . .

Ha! Scratch that! Maybe I'll try counting Walters.

Or maybe not . . . All those Walters in my dream would be more like a **NIGHTMARE!**

Friday:

IT'S HERE! IT'S HERE!!

IT'S HERE!!!

I set my Mega-Bleep-Digi-Clock to wake me up super early. **AAAHH!** I can't wait to get to school and nab a front-row seat for the gala assembly. **YEAH!!!!**

TODAY IS FINALLY HERE!!!!

I'll let you know how it all goes,

my Trainee Menaces!

Some . . . something . . . something has gone HORRIBLY wrong . . .

It's . . . it's TERRIBLE!

I . . . I . . . I don't know what happened.

I never imagined that I'd . . . I'd . . . Ugh!

I can't concentrate. My head is spinning with the shock . . .

OK, BREATHE, DENNIS . . .

↓

(BREATHE!)

Let me try to explain . . . →

I got to school with loads of time before the gala and made sure I had a seat right at the front. **I was so excited!** I'd put the vomit-flavoured sweets into a little box and wrapped it up with some of the gift paper that Mum had saved from last Christmas.

I was going to give it to Walter when he won. It would have been **BRILLIANT** watching his piggy little face pucker up as he chewed, but . . . but . . . I . . .

UGH!

FOCUS, DENNIS!

The hall was packed! Almost the whole town had squeezed inside to watch Walter get his place at Posh Street School. There were even reporters from the *Beanotown Bugle* and photographers to take loads of pictures of him.

It all went so fast . . .

Before I knew it, Headmaster and Mrs Creecher were on stage welcoming Phyllida Snoot, the Headmistress of Posh Street School, and she looked like the most boring adult in the History of Boring Adults. I remember thinking Walter must be barmy to want to go to her school . . .

She was holding an envelope in her hand . . . and she opened it . . . and . . . and . . .

then she said it . . .

At first, I thought there must have been some mistake . . . or maybe someone was playing a prank. **I got _0_ in my test . . .**

There was no way I'd won the place at Posh Street School.

Before I even had time to open my mouth, Walter started screaming. He turned the colour of an

angry tomato,

then started

stomping up

and down on

the spot and

shouting.

NO! I WON!
I WON!
I WON!

For a minute I almost relaxed. Of course it was just a mix-up and it was obvious that Walter was telling the truth . . . but then I saw Mrs Creecher and Headmaster, and I knew!

IT WAS NO MISTAKE AT ALL!

THIS . . .

    HAD . . .

        BEEN . . .

            PLANNED!!!

That look on their faces . . . I'd seen it before.
It was the same one that Walter always pulls
when he thinks he's beaten me at something.

The look of a **devious Softy!**

MRS CREECHER
AND HEADMASTER

HAD OUT-MENACED ME!!!

In a flash, I could see exactly what they'd done. Those EVIL, TRICKY, SNEAKY

BUM-FACES

wanted to get rid of me and had lied about the test scores.

Just then I remembered my test paper. I still had it stuffed in my back pocket after I couldn't resist trying one of the vomit sweets from Mr Har Har's and had spat it out into my answers sheet. I ran to the stage and waved it at Miss Snoot, but everyone kept patting me on the back, and shoving me backwards and forwards, and before I could do anything . . .

Mrs Creecher grabbed it!!!

She was just as surprised as I was when she saw I still had my test paper with me. I thought she was going to tear it up (which would have been OK because I could have stuck all the pieces back together with sticky tape from my menacing detective kit), but she didn't . . . SHE STUFFED IT INTO HER MUG OF TEA!

It was completely ruined . . . and it was the only piece of evidence I had to prove that Creech and Headmaster were lying!

Miss Snoot just patted me on the head after
Creecher soaked my test paper and said . . .

Well done,
Dennis.
See you on
Monday.

I should have shouted out.

I should have grabbed her and told her what

Mrs Creecher and Headmaster had done, but

I was too shocked. She was gone before I'd

even had time to think about it and now

there's nothing I can do.

Walter blames me, of course. He thinks I did it just to upset him and tore his test paper up in a fit of tears and howling, so I can't even ask my arch-enemy for help.

But Creecher CAN'T win!

Old Dreary Drawers can't beat the
PRANKMASTER GENERAL . . . can she?

| . . . | . . . | . . .

I'M GOING TO POSH STREET SCHOOL!!!

Dear Trainee Menaces,

By the time you read this, my brain will have turned to slop and my head will have exploded into a thousand pieces from the complete and utter misery I feel after being beaten by a **BUM-FACE**!

Don't forget to keep up your menacing training! Please put **hot, HOT, HOT** chilli powder in Mrs Creecher's tea and replace Headmaster's toothpaste with shampoo . . .

or just poo . . .

I can see a bright light ahead . . .

I'm fading . . .

Dennis

10.30 a.m.: Euuurrghhh!

I'm not dead! I was certain I'd never wake up

again after getting the shock of my life

yesterday. What am I going to do?

11 a.m.: THIS IS TERRIBLE!

Mum and Dad are completely over the moon

about me getting into Posh Street School. They

think it's the best thing that's ever happened

to our family. To make things even worse, Mum

has taken me out shopping to buy a new school

uniform for Posh Street. A UNIFORM?!

How am I going to cope in a school of Softies?

I'll go mad!

This is a nightmare!

IT HAS TO BE!

11.32 a.m.: I'M STILL ALIVE!

Any minute now . . . any minute now, my brain is going to explode and I'll never be able to even think about Softies, or uniforms, or Posh Street School again . . .

11.40 a.m.: Any minute now . . .

11.51 a.m.: AGH! I'm starting to panic.

We're in the school-uniform shop and I don't seem to be dying for some reason! If I don't pop my clogs soon, I'll have to try a uniform on and . . .

12 noon: LOOK AT ME! JUST LOOK AT ME!

I never thought I'd see the day that I'd be standing around in a smart uniform.

I LOOK LIKE A TOTAL BUM-FACE!

I'll never be able to show my face in Beanotown again after this. No Menace will ever want to build a fort at the junkyard or play secret agents in our top-secret tree house with me again . . . **I'll be laughed at by anyone who isn't a Softy.**

2 p.m.: I never thought I'd say this, my Menacing Mates, but I'm ~~scared~~

~~sc~~ared

sc~~ww~~ared

SCARED!!!

On the way back from the school-
uniform shop, Mum drove past
Posh Street School to have a
look. It's definitely the kind
of place where really, really,
REALLY booky monsters
would live. Like a nightmare
library . . . or a prison
. . . or a **PRISON
LIBRARY!**

POSH STREET

I can't go in there!!!

What if I... what if
I turn into a **Softy?**

I've narrowly avoided getting brainwashed
by hordes of **booky-bum-faces**, but I've
NEVER been in a whole school full of them!

THIS IS THE
WORST DAY
OF MY LIFE!

Sunday

AGH! I WAS WRONG . . .

THIS is the worst day of my life!

It's even more horrible than yesterday . . .

Mum and Dad are SO happy.

WHAT'S WRONG WITH THEM?!?!

They keep humming to themselves and grinning

at me. It's getting creepy. I even heard them

talking in the kitchen . . .

Maybe Posh Street School will teach Dennis how to behave!

He'll be good and polite in no time.

Don't they know their only son is about to be lost forever? Don't they know that the next time they see him after tomorrow he'll probably be wearing socks with sandals and be a **butterfly-watching bore?**

The only one who seems to realize the **TERRIBLE** danger I'm in is Gnasher. He keeps walking in little circles around me, looking all sad and frightened. I tried to get him to tear my school uniform to shreds, but he couldn't stomach the sickening taste of Softy, poor thing. I can't blame him really.

This will be the last entry in my menacing manuals that you ever read . . .

GOODBYE, MY MENACING MATES.

Never stop menacing when I'm gone and make sure you take care of Ghasher for me.

7 a.m.: OK, so I'm still here . . . Mum woke me up this morning with a huge plate of Poppin' Jammy Sour-Candy Toaster Tarts for breakfast. She's so bouncy and skippy and hummy that she still hasn't noticed how miserable I am. I can't bring myself to take a single bite . . .

Me . . . **THE INTERNATIONAL MENACE OF MYSTERY** . . . turning down Poppin' Jammy Sour-Candy Toaster Tarts . . . AND THEY'RE THE BUBBLEGUM-FLAVOURED ONES WITH JELLY BEANS AND CHOCCO SPRINKLES STUCK ALL OVER THEM!

It's over . . .

THE PRANKMASTER GENERAL IS <u>FINISHED!</u>

MY MENACING REIGN IS AT AN <u>END!</u>

I'm certain of it now. There's **NO WAY** I'll last even one day at Posh Street School. I'll probably step inside the front door and instantly start skipping and singing. My Menace's brain won't be able to cope with the poisonous fumes of stinky Softy and boredom and . . . and . . .

UGH!

I can't think about it!

Hmmm . . . so I'm STILL not a Softy,
but that doesn't mean that things aren't
THE WORST. Mum and Dad just dropped
me outside the front of the school. It makes
Number 13 Frightville Avenue, the scariest
house in all of Beanotown, look like a cutesy—
wutesy cottage.

Before I could even think about making one
final dash for the junkyard and spending
the rest of my life living off half—eaten
SLOPPER-GNOSHER-GUT-BUSTIN'
BURGERS, Miss Snoot showed up.

It's the first time I'd got a really good look
at her close up . . . **YIKES!** She's like a
cactus in a cardigan!

Pointy glasses – only the most evil, booky types wear POINTY GLASSES

Weasel face

Honking great nose for sniffing out Menaces

Boring, bum-face clothes

Extra tappy shoes for angry toe-tapping

You can tell she's the kind of lady who does sums for fun at the weekends. I bet her and Mrs Creecher would be **BEST** friends.

Before I could even wave to Mum and Dad, or give Gnasher a goodbye hug, she grabbed me by the arm and pulled me through the front door.

IT'S TOO AWFUL, my Menacing Mates. I was wrong about the whole place stinking of **BUM and BOREDOM**. No . . . it smells of something much, much,

MUCH WORSE.

From the second that weaselly old Snoot dragged me through the front door, my nose started stinging and I knew right then . . . After all, I'd recognize that pong anywhere after the Softy horrors I've seen in the past . . .

Posh Street School smells of **FLOWERS!**

WHAT AM I GOING TO DO?

I could have coped with the stink of bottom and books for a little while . . . I've been around Walter and his bum-faced chums, Dudley and Bertie, for years. **But flowers?!?!**

SUMS ARE FUN!

They're everywhere!!!

SOFTIES, IN THEIR HUNDREDS!!! It's

like a nightmare . . . a flower-scented,

drippy **NIGHTMARE!** Everyone

here has names like Mungo, Cedric,

Flossy and Leonora! **LEONORA?**

I thought that was a type of

washing powder!

9.33 a.m.: I just saw a boy take one look at his timetable of classes and burst out crying.

I HAVE A FOUR-HOUR MATHS CLASS THIS AFTERNOON!

TIMETABLE

Four hours of maths!?!

No wonder he was crying. I think I'd curl up and cry forever if I had a four-hour maths class. For a second I thought he might be another Menace who'd somehow ended up here by some dreadful stroke of bad luck, like me . . . but then I realized he was crying

BECAUSE FOUR HOURS
WASN'T ENOUGH!

Everyone here is

STARK RAVING BONKERS!

9.40 a.m.: Right, my Trainee Menaces, this is it . . . I've just been handed my class timetable by one of the teachers. I feel sick. I can't bring myself to unfold it and have a look.

My hands are shaking . . . / . . / . . .

Come on, Dennis, you're not defeated yet. Mrs Creecher is probably the most boring person in the world and if you can cope with her mind-numbing classes without turning into a Softy I'm sure this won't be any more of a challenge. I just need to look on the bright side: at least Walter isn't here . . .

OK, here goes . . .

POSH STREET

OVA ET LARDUM

	1	**2**	**LUNCH**
MONDAY	Maths and Money-counting	⟨Love Poetry⟩ ← *NOoooo!*	*About time! I'm starving!*
TUESDAY	Morris Dancing ↑ *Morris who?*	Cross-country Skipping	Cryptic-crossword Solving
WEDNESDAY	Garland-weaving and Pottery	~~Butterfly~~ TIGER-watching from a Safe Distance	Cribbage
THURSDAY	*Paper-plane-making* ~~Napkin-folding~~ for Beginners	Posture and Good Manners *Fart!*	Board Games *Bored games more like!*
FRIDAY	Watercolours ~~(Beige Only)~~ *Red and black!!!*	Letter-writing	~~Chess~~ *Cheese!*

3	4	AFTER SCHOOL
Shallow-water Synchronized Paddling	The Art of Soufflés	Choir Practice
The History of ~~Stamp-collecting~~ Flower-STOMPING!	Super-safe Science	~~Tiddlywinks~~ Piddlywinks!
Extra-complicated Spelling	Communicating with Commoners	Elocution Class *What?!*
Low-impact Rambling	The Art of ~~Dinner~~ Parties Menacing	Debating Practice (No arguments allowed)
Quality Caviar Recognition YUCK! Why no burgers?	Rapscallion Survival and Self-defence	Ballet is for Softies

NOOOOOOOO!!!!

Midnight:

My merry band of Menaces, I'll **NEVER** make it! Today was a **BATTLEFIELD OF BORING!** It just kept going from bad to worse.

I knew it was going to be tough . . . **REALLY TOUGH** . . . but I **NEVER** imagined so much horror.

I didn't know boredom could exist on such a massive scale!

I'm **serious!!!** If I had a bored-o-meter and brought it into the class with me, it would self-destruct into a thousand tiny pieces.

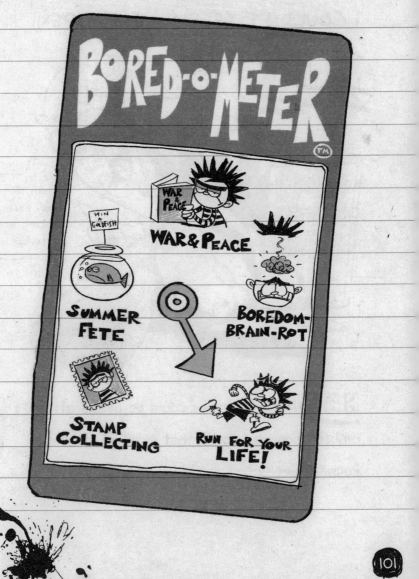

At one point in my morning maths class, I had
to prop a book up in front of me and pretend I
was reading, just so I could take a nap.
I COULDN'T KEEP MY EYES OPEN
and it was only 10 a.m.!

I say, old
chap! You're
missing all
the fun!

HA! Who knew books could be useful after
all? If I managed to do that in all my classes,
Posh Street School would be a breeze.

It was in my next class that I had a

SUPER-GENIUS idea. We were

supposed to be writing love poems

and I could feel panic setting in.

Love poems are for slobber-choppsy

teachers and wobbly old ladies . . .

NOT MENACES!

I was about to abandon hope of ever

making mischief again when I thought

of it . . .

I decided I would try to get myself

kicked out of school. That bunch of

Wet-Lettuces would soon send me

packing if I was naughty.

It's all so horrible, my Menacing Mates . . . and it's not just me I'm worried about, you know! I'm scared for you too.

My diaries have NEVER been filled with so much Softy activity. What if it rots your brain? You're obviously MEGA-BRAVE for reading this far without running away and hiding. You're clearly a first-class Menace.

Things went from bad to worse at lunchtime.
It was **SERIOUSLY** disgusting . . .

I couldn't eat any of that posh stuff! I just
had to sit there while all the other kids ate
platefuls that looked more like a sloppy
garden than a proper meal. YUCK!!!

And anyway . . . even if I did want to eat, there were so many knives and forks I wouldn't have known where to start. I had a bit of a sneaky think, though, and I'm pretty sure I've figured it out.

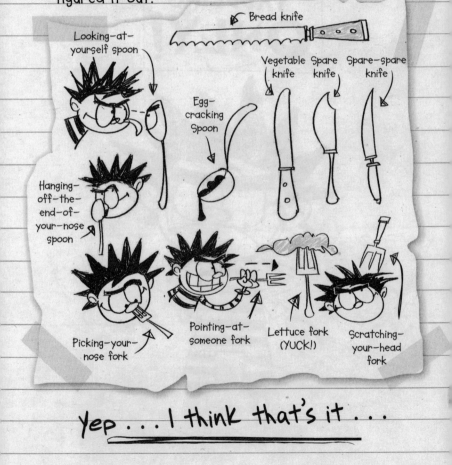

Bread knife

Looking-at-yourself spoon

Egg-cracking spoon

Vegetable knife

Spare knife

Spare-spare knife

Hanging-off-the-end-of-your-nose spoon

Picking-your-nose fork

Pointing-at-someone fork

Lettuce fork (YUCK!)

Scratching-your-head fork

yep . . . I think that's it . . .

The afternoon was a complete disaster. First,
we had swimming. I was quite looking forward to
that until . . .

Then we made soufflés!

What's a soufflé?!?!
I still don't know and I made one!

Agh!

Anyway, you probably guessed that it was a complete and utter **SNOOZEFEST**. Especially when, after all that, they made us go to choir practice and sing songs about lambs prancing through a meadow.

That was the moment I knew, my Trainee Menaces. Those prancing farm animals were the last straw . . . well, that and the French onion soup the canteen served for dinner . . .

I've lasted one day, but I can't stick it any more in this Dullsville. I'll catch **Boredom-Brain-Rot** any minute now if I don't do something quickly.

So . . . I'm going to plot my escape and get out, even if it's the last thing I do!

It's torture here. Everyone brushed their teeth, got changed into their teddy-bear onesies and were in bed by **7 p.m.**

EVEN MY BABY SISTER, BEA, DOESN'T GO TO BED THAT EARLY!

It's like the whole world has gone completely nuts. Where was my bedtime bowl of Double Fatties' double-fat ice cream? Where was my mug of chocco milk? **Don't Softies EVER have fun???**

DOUBLE FATTIES
DOUBLE FAT ICE CREAM

BUT . . . all my crawly-classmates going to bed so early did give me time to come up with a cunning plan. They don't call me **DENNIS THE MENACE** for nothing!

As soon as I get up tomorrow, **OPERATION SNOOTY SCHOOL ESCAPE** is on . . .

6 a.m.: Check . . . check . . .

This is Dennis coming to you live from Posh Street School for **BORING-BOOKY-BUM-FACES**.

Today's the day, my Menacing Mates!

I've got my escape plan all figured out. I can't spend another **MIND-NUMBING** day in here!

Menacing Lesson no. 2229:

All Menaces need to make a quick escape from time to time.

Keep your eyes peeled and your brain alert. Anything can help you escape if you use it properly.

I'll keep you posted . . .

No chance yet. I was so hungry from not eating lunch or dinner yesterday that I got completely distracted by the mountains of toast in the canteen this morning. All the other kids were eating truffled quails' eggs with caviar (yuck!), so there was loads of bread for me . . .

LOADS!!!

FINALLY SOMETHING THAT ISN'T POISONOUS TO MENACES! There wasn't a single Poppin' Jammy Sour-Candy Toaster Tart to be had, but I didn't care. I ate about eight slices of toast and butter and did the most AMAZING mega-burp afterwards. It was so good the boy on the next table fainted into his breakfast. Ha! It's the little things that make the menacing life worthwhile!

8.20 a.m.:

FAILED ESCAPE ATTEMPT NO. 1...

SO CLOSE!!!

I was just leaving the school canteen when I noticed one of the teachers arrive and leave the front door slightly open. My heart nearly jumped up into my mouth. I checked no one was about and made a dash for it. **Agh!** I got to the door without anybody seeing me, yanked it open and . . .

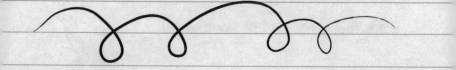

Snoot caught me. Old Cactus-Pants herself . . .

She had no idea what I was up to, though, so

there's still a chance. **Ha!** Teachers are

SOOOOOOOOOO
STUPID!

11.45 a.m.:

FAILED ESCAPE ATTEMPT NO. 2 . . .

We were out on the school footy field, doing cross-country skipping, when I spotted a bush near the end of the track. Just as I was passing, I grabbed the opportunity and dived into it.

For a second I thought I'd got away with it until some Softy girl called Tabitha jumped in after me and tried to give me first aid . . .

I saw him fall, the poor dear.

116

Before I knew it, the whole class had
gathered round to help me up. Why do
Softies always have to try to be helpful?
Don't they realize helpful people can be a
TOTAL pain in the bum?

I'm going to need to think big if I'm going
to escape from this place.

I need something **AMAZING** . . .
something **cool** and **menace-tastic**
that can get me out of here without any
teachers . . . or Softy students . . .
stopping me.

Hmmmm . . .

MEGA-ESCAPE ATTEMPT NO. 1

Try to eat lots of cabbage at lunchtime without being sick . . .

then fill all my pillowcases with mega-farts tonight at bedtime and float out through the dormitory window.

FAILED! Couldn't swallow the cabbage.

1 p.m.: Ok, so that didn't work. Time to try something else.

We have our History of Stamp-collecting lesson after lunch. I can barely bring myself to write the words . . . SO BORING!!!

THINK, DENNIS, THINK!

2.30 p.m.:

HAHA!

I'm a MENACING MASTERMIND.

I managed to stuff my socks full of spoons
from the canteen during lunchtime. Well,
I didn't have anything else to do . . .

They served us mung-bean fritters with
alfalfa dip . . . **BLEEEUURGH!**
If I don't get some proper food soon,
I won't need to worry about escaping.
I'll starve to death and dry up like a . . .
like a mung-bean fritter!!!

Now I just need to get through the rest of
the day without anyone noticing my secret
spoon stash . . .

11 p.m.: I've got to get out tonight, my merry band of Menaces. Today was even more **BORING** than the day before and I'll never survive garland-weaving class tomorrow morning.

It's now or never!

Here's what I've come up with so far . . .

MEGA-ESCAPE ATTEMPT
NO. 2

 Wait for all the other Softy kids to fall asleep.

 Tie spare bedsheets from the dormitory cupboard together and use them as a rope to get out of the window.

 Sneak over to the flower beds in the schoolyard.

Right . . . I've made it this far without being spotted. Now all I have to do is . . .

1 Use the **spoons** to <u>dig down</u> through the flower bed.

2 <u>Tunnel</u> under the **playground**, towards the surrounding wall.

3 Dig deeper and **Wriggle** under the wall.

4 POP back up on the other side.

5 <u>Run</u> to
Beanotown Burgers.

6 <u>Stuff face</u> with
Slopper-Gnosher-
Gut-Bustin' Burgers.

7 <u>Go home</u> and eat ice-cream
with Gnasher.

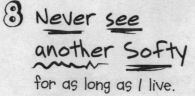

8 <u>Never see</u>
<u>another Softy</u>
for as long as I live.

<u>Midnight:</u> Don't get too excited, my Menacing Mates . . . I'm back in the dormitory.

It was going **REALLY WELL** . . . **UGH!** This is **TERRIBLE!**

I must have taken a wrong turn or something.

I was digging for **AGES** . . . and, just when I thought I was about to break through the ground on the other side of the school walls, I came up in the herb garden at the back of the kitchen.

I was so confused that I didn't even notice a figure standing over me at first.

It was Miss Snoot. She was making her last rounds of the school before popping off to bed.

Well, don't start panicking, my Menacing
Mates. Just remember whose diary you're
reading. I know Old Snoot caught me red-
handed trying to tunnel out of school, but no
one can tell fibs like I can.

> Evening, Miss Snoot.
> I just couldn't sleep
> until I'd been down
> here to check on the
> herbs. I was singing to
> the roots . . . They
> love it!

The gristly old pilchard believed every word of
it. She kept going on about how impressed she
was with my generosity and caring.

Ha! FOOLED HER!

Wednesday

8.30 a.m.: GAH! I might have got away with my failed tunnelling last night, but I'M STILL HERE. I'm running out of ideas and we've got garland-weaving class first thing this morning . . .

HELP!!!

10 a.m.: Dying . . . Made garlands of flowers . . . Can't see properly . . .

so much pink!

12.30 p.m.: If I don't menace something soon, I'm going to lose my mind.

I'M SO MISERABLE . . .
AND STARVING!

We've been butterfly-watching . . .
BUTTERFLIES! FLOATY, FLAPPY,

CUTESY
BUTTERFLIES!!!

I tried catching a few to remind me of my squished-bug collection back at home, but it didn't make me feel better.

Midnight:

My Menace's heart is breaking,

Trainee Menaces. I was lying in bed, half awake, half dreaming about Greasy-Battered-Turkey-Twists from Bash Street School canteen, when I heard a weird noise. It sounded really far away and was **SUPER** familiar, but I thought it was in my dream at first. Then, as it kept on going, I realized what it was.

I ran to the window and I could hear my best dog-pal howling at the moon. I could imagine the tree house in my back garden at home with Gnasher standing in the doorway.

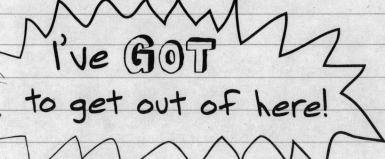

I've GOT to get out of here!

I can't stick around in this misery museum when my poor dog is missing his menacing master. Before I knew it, I was howling back at him across town.

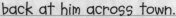

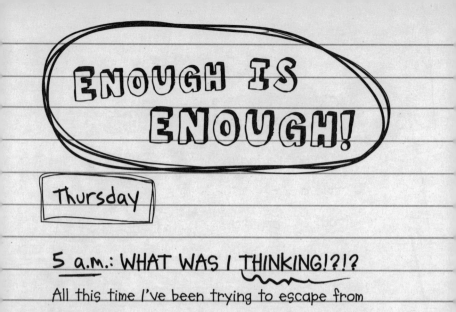

ENOUGH IS ENOUGH!

Thursday

5 a.m.: WHAT WAS I THINKING!?!?

All this time I've been trying to escape from

this BUM-FACED school by myself when I have

the best, BEST, **BESTEST** Menace Squad

living outside the walls!

I've set my Mega-Bleep-Digi-Clock to wake

me up before the rest of my Softy classmates,

then I'm going to sound the menacing alarm.

A few notes folded into paper aeroplanes

should do the trick . . .

CALLING
ALL MENACES!

Your menacing leader is in **TERRIBLE** trouble and needs your help. If I don't get out of Posh Street School soon, my brain will fry and I'll become a disgusting, mutant, Softy beast.

If you are cool, smart, brave, funny or just plain **AMAZING**, you won't ignore this message and miss out on the adventure of a lifetime.

It's time for a **SNOOTY** School Escape!

Come tonight at midnight . . .

Dennis

5.30 a.m.: I wrote the same message about a trillion times and threw them in every direction from the dormitory window, my Menacing Mates.

That has to work . . .

IT JUST HAS TO!

8.30 a.m.: **YIKES!** After I convinced
old Cactus-Pants that I was singing to the
herbs the other night, she made me STAR
PUPIL in assembly this morning. Me . . .
the star pupil in a Softy school!?!

This is bad news . . . Please, PLEASE,
PLEASE, PLEASE, PLEASE,

PLEASE

LET ONE OF MY NOTES BE FOUND BY
A MENACE! I'm not sure how much longer
I can last.

11 p.m.: No reply yet, but Menaces always find a way to get back to you if they get a secret note.

Come on . . .

come on . . .

COME ON . . .

12.20 p.m.:

Still nothing.

1 p.m.:

Parsley and lettuce soup for lunch . . .

CAN'T . . .

TAKE . . .

MUCH . . .

MORE . . .

140

1.12 p.m.: Not sure why, but I'm feeling the urge to stroll among the flower beds. **AGH!** I think . . .

I THINK I'M TURNING!

I . . . I . . . I think I'm longing for a flower-strewn meadow. I suddenly **REALLY** want to comb my hair and brush my teeth . . .

NO!

I'M SAVED!!!

HA! THE BEST THING JUST HAPPENED, MY MERRY BAND OF MENACES! Just as I was starting to break into a gentle skip towards the garden, a piece of paper, all squidged up with spit, flew over the playground wall and hit me right in the face.

There's nothing more menacy than a spitball from a pea-shooter and it was just what I needed to snap me out of it.

BUT that's not the best part!

When I un-squidged the paper, there was a message written on it.

We're coming tonight! Gran x

I knew I could count on my **BRILLIANT**, **MENACE-TASTIC** gran. She's one of the oldest Menaces in all of Beanotown and there's nobody better to help you out of a Softy scrape.

Here goes, my Trainee Menaces. Don't you dare stop reading or put this diary down. I have a feeling things are about to get

SUPER FUN!

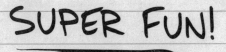

11.50 p.m.: I'm so excited, I could

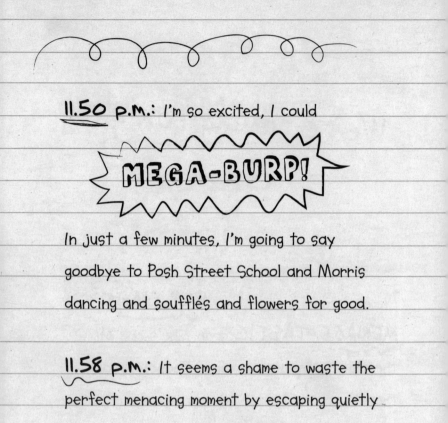

MEGA-BURP!

In just a few minutes, I'm going to say goodbye to Posh Street School and Morris dancing and soufflés and flowers for good.

11.58 p.m.: It seems a shame to waste the perfect menacing moment by escaping quietly and I'm pretty sure a distraction wouldn't hurt while I make my getaway . . .

Hmmmmmm . . .

11.59 p.m.: <u>HAHA!</u> I can hear Gran's Charley Davidson motorbike coming from the other side of town.

GET READY,
MY MENACING MATES!

I'll tell you all about it when I'm out of this dump . . .

Oh, and I found the perfect distraction . . .

11.30 a.m.: WE DID IT!

My merry band of Menaces, I wish you could
have been there to see what happened last
night. It was the BEST NIGHT OF MY LIFE.
I've never seen such an amazing, brilliant,
INCREDIBLE marvel of menacing.

I'll tell you all about it . . .

Just as I set off the panic alarm, I watched
Gran's Charley Davidson do a KILLER jump
over the school wall. It was the most impressive
motorbike jump I'd ever seen, and it didn't take
me long to see how her bike had enough turbo
power to leap so high.

HA! My **BRILLIANT** little sister must have found the rest of my packet of fart pellets!

In seconds, the whole school was awake and people were running this way and that, shouting:

There's a Menace on the loose!

We're under attack!

Ha! The Softies didn't know what had hit them.

I ran out to the playground just in time to see the rest of Beanotown's Menaces arrive. It was one of the GREATEST sights

EVER!

In no time at all, the whole of my Menace Squad was assembled and ready for battle. After all, you didn't think we were just going to leave without causing a little bit of mayhem, did you?

Haha! It was brilliant . . . Softies were screaming and running about like headless chickens.

It felt so good to be menacing again . . . and there was no way I was getting out of there until I showed old Snoot just how much of a Menace her star pupil was. What kind of Menaces would we be if we didn't leave some chaos behind us?

Gran went inside to herd the Softies out . . .

And the Bash Street Kids menaced the classrooms . . .

That was
when Miss Snoot
showed up.

WHAT ON EARTH
IS GOING ON?!

She stared at me like a bull about to charge

and started screaming.

Get away from my herb
garden, you horrible little
guttersnipe! I should have
known you'd be a rapscallion.
YOUR HAIR ISN'T NEAT!

Then it was my turn . . .

Well, you've got
a BUM-FACE!

At that moment, I gave the signal and Bea dealt with Miss Snoot's BORING herbs.

Haha! It was brilliant!

But then . . . the **BEST** bit of all happened.

Before Miss Snoot could blow her bonce off with shock, everyone started pointing at the sky, yelling and shouting.

I looked up and . . . and . . .

HA! YOU'LL NEVER GUESS
WHAT WE SAW!

WAS IT A BIRD?

WAS IT AN INTERSTELLAR
BUM-FACED COMET?

NO! IT WAS WALTER!!!!

I'd never seen anything so funny in my life.

Walter had built himself some sort of gliding

thingummybob and had flown straight over the

wall of Posh Street School.

He landed in the middle of the

playground with the smarmiest of

smarmer-smiles on his face.

Then . . . Ha!

I can barely write it, it was so

HILARIOUS!

Then he saw that his beloved

bum-face school had been turned

into a Menacing Wonderland by

THE PRANKMASTER GENERAL

and his band of merry Menaces.

NOOOOOOOOO!!

I honestly think it was the best moment of my life! HA!

But . . . I wasn't about to stick around in that boring, booky school any longer. Walter could keep what was left of Posh Street School.

It was time to go. Gran threw me a dustbin
lid and the end of a piece of rope and we
were out of there quicker than you can say
'Old Mother Cactus—Pants' . . .

Ahhhh . . . the good times . . .

It won't surprise you to know that I've been officially kicked out of Posh Street School.

HAHA! Miss Shoot was so angry about her herb garden she gave the entire school detention just to make herself feel better!

You should have seen Headmaster's and Mrs Creecher's faces today when I showed up back at Bash Street School.

They looked terrified! They thought I was going to cause a ton of trouble to get them back for out-menacing me and having me sent away to snooty school, but I didn't . . .

I was **SUPER** nice! In fact, I gave them some extra-special sweets to show them just how much I'd missed them . . .

WHY NOT DO YOUR OWN MENACE JOURNAL?

I've menaced my diary . . . now it's time to menace yours!

Join *The Beano* comic's front-page legend as he guides you through everything you need to know to create a book just like his. Your teacher will hate it!

COLLECT ALL THE BOOKS IN THE DIARY OF DENNIS THE MENACE SERIES!